The Shrieking Face

That was the moment when Kevin fell out of his tree with a blood-curdling scream, Mum ran to the door to rescue him, and Rosco burst in, leaping excitedly with muddy paws on to the pile of freshly-ironed pillowcases. As Mrs Lang bore in a grazed and loudly-wailing Kevin, Angus decided to flee to his bedroom. On the way, he shouted defiantly from the staircase:

'Anyway, my peace picture was the best, even with you lot in it!'

'And that's enough of your cheek!' retorted Mrs Lang.

Hazel Townson

The Shrieking Face

Illustrated by Tony Ross

Beaver Books

For Audrey Adams

A Beaver Book
Published by Arrow Books Limited
17–21 Conway Street, London W1P 6JD

An imprint of the Hutchinson Publishing Group

London Melbourne Sydney Auckland
Johannesburg and agencies throughout the world

First published by Andersen Press 1984
Beaver edition 1986

Text © Hazel Townson 1984
Illustrations © Andersen Press 1984

Set in Baskerville

Made and printed in Great Britain
by Anchor Brendon Ltd
Tiptree, Essex

ISBN 0 09 941310 8

Chapter 1

Angus Lang crackled with rage. He plunged his paintbrush into thick black paint then daubed a great, shrieking face across the middle of his picture. It was the face of his teacher, Mrs Crake, with her mouth wide open in a nasty, ugly shout.

'Serve her right if she recognises herself,' thought Angus. For that was just how Mrs Crake looked when she was going on at him all the time, nag, nag, nag!

'Angus Lang, I won't tell you again to stop talking!'

'Angus Lang, you are capable of much better work than this!'

'Angus Lang . . . Angus Lang . . . .'

Slap, slap, the lines on the picture grew thicker, until Angus began to feel really good, as though he had just kicked a vital goal or speared a dragon. He sat back to admire the face, then added, with a final, vicious dab, a great black spot on the end of the nose. Perfect!

The picture was supposed to be called 'Peace'. It was something special they were all doing for a big competition. And in fact, until Mrs Crake had rattled him, Angus had been enjoying his own interpretation of that word . . . green countryside, ending in a colourful garden where his dad was digging, his kid brother Kevin was playing with Rosco the dog, and his mum sat knitting in a deck chair. Now this happy scene looked as if it had been gobbled up by Satan himself.

The moment's triumph passed, and reaction set in. Dread crept into Angus's stomach and lay there like a heavy load of stone-cold fish and chips. What would old Corny say when she saw what he'd done? She might tear his painting up, or stand him in a corner, or send him to the Head. But worse that any of these things was the fear of Corny's clever, biting sarcasm which could reduce even a rugby front row forward to the size of a Tom Thumb.

Angus leaned across his painting, circled his arms protectively about it and willed the face to disappear. But of course it didn't, and it was only a matter of time before Mrs Crake loomed up behind him, prised him backwards—and gasped!

There was a moment's silence, during which the whole of Angus's life passed through his drowning mind. Then Mrs Crake said: 'Why, that's wonderful! That's simply wonderful!'

What did she mean? Was this a new sarcastic turn? But no; Mrs Crake was really pleased with the picture. In fact, she seemed almost moved to tears as she tenderly gathered up the wet painting and transferred it to her table.

'Well, Angus Lang, I always said you had it in you. Look, class! This picture says in a few simple lines what the whole Campaign for Nuclear Disarmament has been trying to say for years. There looms the face of the monster which threatens the peace of the world. We all know what that monster is, and how it hangs over everthing we do . . . .' At this point a definite dewy glitter could be detected in Mrs Crake's eye, and it was just as well that the bell went for the end of afternoon school.

Angus ran all the way home, anxious to flee the guilt of having turned old Corny's brain. That must be what he had done. All that rubbish she'd talked about his picture! The only monster Angus had seen hanging over everything he did was Mrs Crake herself. She must have recognised her own face, after all, but to ramble on like that about it! She must have gone completely bonkers. Perhaps she would have to see a psychiatrist. Perhaps she'd have to leave school. Great! Yet at the same time, terrible! For it was all Angus's fault.

When Angus arrived home he found Rosco the dog in disgrace for chewing a sofa cushion, his kid brother Kevin all bandaged up after a fall, and his mother shouting at his dad who had just come home early because the factory was out on strike.

'I don't know what gets into you lot these days! You're always out on strike. It's bad enough trying to manage on a decent week's wages, never mind strike pay . . . .'

'Exactly!' said Angus's dad, giving Angus a wink. 'Anyway, I notice there's always enough money for Mars bars for our Kevin every time he falls over. You're spoiling that lad rotten, and I don't just mean his teeth.'

'Leave him alone. His knee hurts, doesn't it, Kevvy?'

This was the cue for Kevin to start wailing, so Dad, to change the subject, asked Angus what he'd

been doing at school.

'Drawing a picture of peace,' replied Angus shiftily, not wanting to think too hard about the afternoon's events. 'For a competition. There's a prize for the best.'

'Well, you won't win it, never fear!' his mother butted in. 'You're about as artistic as your dad, and the best thing he's ever likely to draw is the old age pension.'

'If I live that long,' retorted Mr Lang. 'Peace, eh? Well, there's not many of us has much idea what that looks like, I can tell you!'

Chapter 2

'Angus Lang! The Headmaster wants to see you.'

Angus in the middle of next day's robust rush to freedom, came to a pale and shaky halt. Retribution at last! Old Corny had obviously come to her senses and complained. Angus trailed slowly back across the playground, wondering what to say.

'I don't know what came over me!' was his grandma's line whenever she had one of her dizzy turns. 'Just an experiment,' was his mother's excuse when the dinner went wrong. ('If I didn't try something new now and then, you'd only say I was stuck in a rut.') Or there was the time his Uncle Ben painted the front door in red, green and yellow stripes, claiming: 'I just felt like it. What's wrong with a bit of self-expression?'

In the end, Angus said none of these things. He didn't have the chance, for the Headmaster, Mr Drabble, did all the talking.

'Well now, Angus, for once you seem to have covered yourself in glory. That's a very fine picture you've done for the competition. So fine, in fact, that we're sending it forward, as this school's one permitted entry, to the regional finals. What have you got to say to that, eh?'

Angus had nothing to say. He was dumbfounded.

'Peace swallowed up by war,' Mr Drabble went on. 'Or the threat of war, which is nearly as bad. You know, my boy, we may have a winner there. It's a very discerning piece of work; almost a stroke of genius. And I must say I'm glad that it's come from you—from a boy who has hitherto been—(let's face it!)—something of a handful. Lazy, dishonest, inattentive, disruptive . . . .'

This was more like it! Finding himself on familiar ground again, Angus perked up. He even managed a rueful grin as he braced himself for the punishment to come. When the Headmaster finally stood up and reached across his desk to shake Angus's hand, the boy almost flinched. Yet all Mr Drabble said was: 'Congratulations! And let this be the first of many triumphs.'

By the time Angus stumbled out into the corridor he felt weaker, sicker and more confused that he usually did after six of the best. He ambled home in a daze, wondering whether he was the one going crazy, and not Mrs Crake. There was certainly something funny happening. Was this what folks felt like in fairy tales when they'd just had a spell put on them?

When he did get home, he found Rosco shut out for gnawing the table-leg, Kevin halfway up a forbidden tree, and his dad setting off with flask

and sandwiches for the night-shift picket line. Inside the house, Mrs Lang was ironing bad-temperedly, muttering away to herself about poverty, slavery and utter selfishness.

'Hi, Mum! What's for tea?'

'Bread and cheese. And you needn't look like that. Think yourself lucky it's not just bread, what with this dratted strike, and the rates and electric gone up again.'

There was more of the same, but Angus closed his ears and moved over to the telly. Might as well watch the children's programmes until the bread and cheese appeared. He turned the switch and settled down hopefully. After a minute, he realised something was wrong, advanced upon the set and gave it a couple of hearty blows on the right-hand side. This usually worked, but not today. Neither sound nor picture was forthcoming.

'Mum, I think the telly's broken.'

'It had better not be!' Mrs Lang laid down her iron and marched towards the set. Twiddling knobs furiously, she berated first the set and then her son, in ever-mounting fury.

'What do you think you're playing at, you great, clumsy . . .?'

'It wasn't me, Mum! I only turned it on.'

'I saw you clouting it on the side. How many times have I told you not to touch that set? If you want it on, you ask me. I'll do the turning.'

'But you were busy ironing . . . .'

'Ironing? Oh, no!'

Mrs Lang leaped back to the ironing board, but it was too late. A great, brown patch had been scorched in the middle of Mr Lang's best shirt.

This was the moment when Kevin fell out of his tree with a blood-curdling scream, Mum ran to the door to rescue him, and Rosco burst in, leaping excitedly with muddy paws on to the pile of freshly-ironed pillowcases. As Mrs Lang bore in a grazed and loudly-wailing Kevin, Angus decided to flee to his

bedroom. On the way, he shouted defiantly from the staircase:

'Anyway, my peace picture was the best, even with you lot in it!'

'And that's enough of your cheek!' retorted Mrs Lang.

Chapter 3

'There is no doubt at all about my choice,' said the Principal of the College of Art. 'Only one of these pictures really has anything to say. The rest of them are insipid, if competently-painted, little day-dreams.'

'Oh, I don't agree!' objected Mrs Moxton, President of the Amateur Landscape Painters' Club. 'Every one of these pictures has a great deal to say. Look at this one, for instance; an old lady feeding the birds in a park full of flowers. Peaceful old age, enjoying the beauties of nature.'

'Sentimental rubbish! An old woman like that would probably have arthritis, inadequate heating, no proper dinner and only the birds for company. Peace my foot! More like a lull between battles.'

'All right then, what about this picnic scene?'

'My dear lady, I ask you, have you ever had a peaceful picnic, with no flies, wasps, wet grass, cow-pats, forgotten hampers, accidents, boredom, bulls, sudden downpours . . .?'

'Well, we all know life is full of little disappointments, but if you're going to go on like that all the time . . . .'

The chairman of the Regional Selection Panel cleared his throat nervously. 'I think a process of

elimination would be best. Perhaps if we could reduce the number of likely winners to three or four, then take a vote on it . . . .'

There was much more argument, but in the end that was what they did. The Panel members found they were unanimous in disliking at least a dozen pictures. This spurred them on to make further decisions, until in the end only three works of art were left. A final vote was taken, and Angus Lang's picture was declared the regional winner, to go forward to the national finals in London.

'I should just think so!' declared the Principal of the College of Art, who had wasted an afternoon of perfect sketching weather. 'It's a mistake to mix amateur and professional judgements on these occasions.'

'Justice has to be seen to be done,' snapped Mrs Moxton nastily, while the chairman of the Panel dithered about trying to shepherd everyone from the room.

Mr Drabble received the news by telephone within the hour.

'Absolutely delighted to tell you that your school's entry has been chosen.'

The Headmaster danced a little jig about his room. 'What did I say?' he asked himself in the mirror. 'We knew that lad's picture was a winner, didn't we? What an honour for the school! If he wins the national prize, I'll give the whole school a half-day holiday.'

Mr Drabble sent for Angus at once to tell him the glad tidings, but Angus was not in school. Rosco had followed him on to the bus that morning, and Angus had had to take the animal back home. By then he was so late that he dared not face the wrath of Mrs Crake, so he went for a walk by the canal instead, and was actually offered a lift on a barge. Angus knew not to accept lifts from strangers in cars, but no one had ever said anything about barges. The whole thing seemed so tranquil and safe and tempting that he clambered aboard.

The barge was carrying some goods from a local factory to Liverpool, whence they were to be shipped abroad.

'It's a lot cheaper than sending 'em by road,' the bargee told Angus, as he peacefully puffed his pipe. 'Now that everybody's trying to keep their costs down, canals is coming back into their own.' Angus felt that he had now learned more than he would have done in a whole day at school, so he stopped feeling guilty and settled down to enjoy himself. By afternoon, he had come to know the bargee well enough to ask him to write a note, signed 'J. Lang', explaining that Angus had not been feeling very well yesterday, and could his absence please be excused.

'You know, it's a great life this,' said Tom the bargee when the note was finished. 'Nobody to bother you, once you've loaded up. Nice leisurely progress—(See that bird over there? That's a heron that is!)—plenty of fresh air and lovely scenery. What more could you want?'

What, indeed? It was pure escape from all the naggers in the world.

'I wish I'd known how peaceful it was out here,' sighed Angus. 'I could have put you in my picture, heron and all.'

Chapter 4

The great news came through on the breakfast-time bulletin:

'The nationwide children's art competition, organised by PANIC—(the Peace-Among-Nations Inspirational Committee)—has been won by Angus Lang, a pupil of Bordham Primary School. Angus's picture, which has been described as "Quite remarkable!" by Sir Desmond Snubbs, the President of the Royal Academy, will be on view in the Taste Gallery until the end of this month.'

'Turn that noise down!' shouted Angus's mum from the far side of the kitchen, where she was frying bread in fat already speckled brown by yesterday's sausages. 'I can't hear myself think in a morning!'

'Lucky you!' grunted Mr Lang from behind his copy of the *Sun*.

'And where's our Angus? He's going to be late for school, as usual.'

Angus was still in bed, enjoying the tail-end of a dream in which he and Tom, his bargee friend, were sailing along towards a free Amusement Park with a cargo of walnut whips. Angus had managed another lift with Tom yesterday—(twenty miles of glorious canal, then back home on the bus)—other-

wise he would have been in school to receive the advance news of his triumph. As it was, he had no idea what lay in store for him when Rosco finally leapt on to his chest and started to nibble his ear.

Angus rose reluctantly. It would have been nice to take another canal jaunt today, but he knew that Tom was now out of reach until next Friday, when he would pass by on the way to Liverpool once more. School this morning, then. Thinking gloomily ahead, Angus remembered the spelling test that would be coming up straight after prayers. Not only had he forgotten to learn his spellings, but he had also lost the list, so that he could not even steal a quick last-minute glance from inside his hymn-book. Perhaps if he prayed hard instead, he would receive inspiration at the proper time, and even get full marks. Better still, could he force two fingers down his throat and make himself sick? So absorbed was he in these alternatives that he was completely taken aback when his best friend Jeffo, meeting him at the garden gate, slapped him hard on the shoulder and shouted breathlessly, 'Hey, what's it feel like to be famous, then?'

'What are you on about?'

'Oh, come off it! Stop acting modest.'

'Honest, Jeffo, I don't know what you mean.'

The two boys argued at cross purposes all the way to the bus stop, and Angus was still no wiser when the bus arrived. Then what a reception he got! Not only was he man-handled forward to the seat of honour at the front, but the entire bus-load of kids began to sing:

Nice one, Angus, nice one, son!

Nice one, Angus! Let's have another one!

'I think you're all barmy!' he finally managed to groan.

'Hey, he doesn't know! He wasn't in school yesterday.'

'No, he was playing hookey again, the crafty devil.'

'Didn't you even listen to the news this morning, Angus?'

'You've only won that blinking Peace prize, that's all.'

'And got us a holiday next Friday afternoon.'

'And had your picture hung up in a fancy frame in a London gallery.'

Angus's stomach lurched, and he looked around desperately for somewhere to be sick.

'You okay?' asked Jeffo with concern.

'No!'

'But you must be pleased. That prize is five hundred quid and a free trip to London. Boy, what could I do with five hundred quid?'

'My mum'll make me put it in the bank,' said Angus gloomily.

'Well, she'll have to let you have it one day. It might double in interest before then. Anyway, she can't stop you taking the free trip to London.'

'She'll want to go with me,' moaned Angus. 'Look, I'll have to get off the bus and go home.'

'Oh, no you don't! Just take a few deep breaths and you'll be all right. Our whole day depends on you being there. They've got a special assembly planned in your honour, so we'll miss the spelling test for a start. And after that . . . .'

As Jeffo outlined the day, Angus began to feel stranger and stranger, as though he had turned into someone else. All his life he'd been a failure, an infuriating nuisance who brought out the worst in people like his mother and Mrs Crake. How could he suddenly have changed? He remembered the 'magic spell' feeling he'd had before, and thought that it did almost seem like a fairy tale—Frog into Prince, or Woodcutter's Son into King. Angus actually rubbed his eyes and shuddered, as if he felt the magic creeping over him. 'Let's hope it's all going to finish with a "Happy Ever After",' he thought.

Chapter 5

Mr Drabble shuffled the pile of papers in front of him and finally came up with a map. This he handed across his desk to Angus.

'There you are, then. That shows you how to get to the Taste Gallery. I've marked the nearest tube station in red, but of course you can always take a taxi if you're doubtful.'

Angus could not imagine his mother 'wasting good money' on a taxi. On the other hand, he couldn't imagine her on the underground escalators either.

'Couldn't we get the bus, sir?'

Mr Drabble grinned. 'Oh, I wouldn't do that if I were you. They're not like the buses up here, you know, bumbling along and dropping you off obligingly at your own front gate.'

Angus began to look so miserable that Mr Drabble took pity on him.

'Cheer up! You're a celebrity now, you know. What's a little journey across London? Think of all the fuss and glory when you get there, met by Sir Desmond Snubbs himself and I-don't-know-who-else.'

'That's what I am thinking, sir.'

'Angus Lang, I do believe you're scared.'

'Petrified, sir. Honest, I'd rather be one of the angels in the infants' Nativity play.'

Mr Drabble leaned back in his chair and laughed. 'Nonsense, lad! You'll enjoy every minute of it, once you arrive. Most of the others wish they were in your shoes, I can tell you. Why, you'll have no trouble getting a scholarship to art college after all this publicity.'

'But I want to be a bargee, sir.'

'A bargee?' Mr Drabble was astounded. He leaned so far out on the back two legs of his chair that he almost came a cropper.

'It's a great life, sir, floating up and down the canal all day . . . .'

'Ah, yes, that would appeal to you, the promise of a nice, lazy time. But I can assure you it's not like that at all. It's extremely hard work, manoeuvring a barge through locks and under tunnels and such. Anyway, your talent lies in quite another direction. You're a born artist, as Mrs Crake tells me she had long suspected.'

'Rotten old liar!' thought Angus. 'Trying to take all the credit.' Aloud, he said: 'You can be your own boss on the canal, sir. There's nobody to bother you once you've loaded your barge up. And if you're interested in birds, sir . . . .'

Birds indeed!

This interview, Mr Drabble decided, was not going at all the way he had planned it. He gave a business-like cough. 'Yes, well, it's time you went back to your classroom, Angus. You'll feel quite differently after next Friday. Believe me, when you've met Sir Desmond Snubbs you won't give barges another thought. Now, I've sorted out all the information you need for the trip, but if your mother has any further problems, tell her to ring me between four and five, any day this week.'

Without quite knowing how it had been managed, Angus found himself standing alone in the corridor with a bundle of official-looking papers

30

under his arm. He began to walk slowly towards his classroom as if in a trance.

Suddenly, a boy called Billy Schofield appeared in front of him.

'Hi, Angus! All fixed up to meet Lord Snotty-nose, are you?'

Angus Lang crackled with rage. He slapped his papers down into a puddle on the nearest window-sill, grabbed Billy Schofield's right ear, dragged him round in a circle and sent him spinning down the corridor. That was more like it! That had shaken off the magic-spell feeling, once and for all.

Chapter 6

'London? What are you talking about?' snapped Mrs Lang. 'If it's a school trip, you know very well we haven't got the money.'

Angus began to explain all over again. His mother evidently hadn't been listening the first time.

'You mean to say you won that prize, then, after all? Well, there must be some mistake. Somebody with the same name or something; there's plenty of Langs about. You can't draw for toffee.'

'Thanks!' said Angus bitterly.

'Well, you can't. You know you can't. I'm only telling the truth. You'd better go and see Mr Drabble in the morning and sort out what's happened.'

'Maybe I can draw. My picture must be some good if they're hanging it in the Taste Gallery.'

'What?' Mrs Lang let go the spoon with which she had been stirring the stew, and Rosco leapt to lick it clean. 'Are you telling me they're going to hang your picture up in a proper art gallery? Next to rude pictures of folks with nothing on? Well, that's disgusting, that is, and you only a child. I don't know what Mr Drabble's thinking of. Give me those papers!'

Mrs Lang snatched at the soggy bundle of documents and spread them out on the kitchen table. She was still reading, with many 'Oooh's and 'Aaaah's and 'Fancy that!'s, when Angus's dad came in.

'Here, look at these! Our Angus has won that prize he was telling us about. Five hundred pounds, it is! Five hundred pounds! He's to go to London to get presented with it. They've even sent train tickets for two.'

'Good for you, then!' grinned Mr Lang to his son. 'I take my hat off to anyone who can earn five hundred quid in one afternoon. I'll go with you to London, if you like.'

'Oh, no you won't! You've your picket line to think of. Anyway, the Headmaster's letter's addressed to me. The presentation's on a Friday. He'd think you'd be working,' Mrs Lang said pointedly. 'Anyway, it's time I had a day out.'

'Suit yourself.' Mr Lang lost interest and started looking round for the evening paper. 'But you'll have to leave our Kevin at your Emily's. I can't be expected to take him with me up the picket.'

'Our Kevin can come with us.'

Angus's heart lurched with alarm. 'There's only two tickets.'

'I'll pay for him myself. Our Emily will lend me a bit until you get your prize money. It's not every day his brother wins a prize, is it, Kevvy? And we can take him to see Buckingham Palace afterwards. He'll like that, won't you, lovey?'

But before he could answer, Kevin, who had been busy sticking his tongue out at Angus behind his mother's back, fell over the dog and began to cry.

'He's not coming! He'll only spoil everything! Look at him now.'

'What a thing to say about your little brother! You oughta be ashamed.'

'He's always in bother. He'll go and fall over or something just at the important bit, and ruin everything.'

Kevin escaped from his mother's embrace to kick Angus on the shin, then ran back and howled louder than ever.

'Oh, hush, love! Mum'll buy you some nice new clothes for London. How about some of them blue velvet pants from Marks's?'

'What about me?' asked Angus.

'You can wear your school uniform. They'll expect it.'

'Oh, great! It's my prize, so he gets new pants. With my money!'

'You needn't worry, son,' Dad butted in. 'There'll be no new pants in this house for a while. As a matter of fact, that five hundred quid's a Godsend, but it's not for wasting. We're going to need every penny of it. This strike looks like lasting till

next December.'

This news sparked off such a terrible outburst from Mrs Lang that Angus slipped from the house and ran and ran until he was out of earshot.

Chapter 7

Thursday, the day before the presentation, was a bustle of preparation. Mrs Lang gave herself a home perm, which was so much of a disaster that she had to go and borrow a floppy hat from her sister Emily. Then she cleaned her shoes for a solid twenty minutes, never heeding that she had used black polish on brown leather. After that, she packed her enormous handbag with such useful items as bandages, throat pastilles, safety pins, kiss-of-life manual, and a novelty scent-bottle shaped like a revolver. You never knew, in a wicked city like London. Mrs Lang had been to London only once before, and that was because she had forgotten to change at Crewe. She remembered it vividly as a place of wild stampedes, stewed tea, bird-droppings, pouring rain and unobliging porters. Yet for the sake of her son's triumph—(and the five hundred pounds)—she was willing to suffer it all again. A great pile of pressed-beef sandwiches was prepared, spread lavishly with mustard to keep out the cold. To these were added two great flasks of coffee, a bag of home-made coconut pyramids and several packets of cheese-and-onion-flavoured potato crisps. All these goodies were to be consumed on the outward journey, despite the fact that Sir

Desmond Snubbs was to entertain them to a five-course luncheon.

'Our Kevin'll be sick before we even get there,' prophesied Angus gloomily. Yet he felt that even this disaster would not shame him as much as his mother's dreadful appearance. Her hair was hideous, her coat was purple and her borrowed hat was a horrible brick-red. Angus knew he would be ashamed of her—and even more ashamed of being ashamed of his own mother. And all that on top of having won the prize by false pretences in the first place!

Angus was sent to bed early with instructions to 'get a good night's sleep', his mother threatening to call him nice and early, so as to have time to examine his ears and fingernails.

'Just you get up right away in the morning, no messing about!'

Angus trailed miserably to his room, wishing only that he might fall asleep at once and, in the fashion of Rip Van Winkle, not wake up again until the whole thing was ancient history. Yet when he did sleep, he wished he hadn't. For then he squirmed and turned in hot and sticky dread, the wild shapes of a nightmare looming round his struggling form. Sir Desmond Snubbs had turned out to be a wicked giant who chased Angus and finally threw him to the sharks in the icy depths of

the river Thames, having first hung Kevin and Mrs Lang round Angus's neck to weight him down. Dawn was actually beginning to seep through the curtains when an exhausted, terrified Angus finally awoke. He lay there trembling for a while, his poor brain in a turmoil... until inspiration finally struck! Of course! There was one way out of his dilemma; why hadn't he thought of it before? It was so simple, too. Suddenly, Angus smiled.

'He's gone!' yelled Mrs Lang, storming into Angus's room a while later to see why he hadn't responded to her rousing shouts. She rushed hysterically through the house, banging doors and slamming cupboards.

'Where's he gone? We've lost him! He's run off!'

When Mr Lang finally appeared in rumpled pyjamas, he was seized, pushed, dragged and shaken by his wife, who screamed at him to 'Do something, can't you? Don't just stand about. He's supposed to be collecting that five hundred pounds.'

In the end, mostly to shut his wife up, Mr Lang telephoned the police to see if they had news of any accidents or runaway boys. They had not, but once their interest had been aroused they did not intend to leave the matter there. Very soon, a sergeant came round to the house.

Angus's fame had spread. The sergeant knew all about the lad's prize picture, and was sure this was the reason for his disappearance. Could it be nerves, he asked Angus's mother? Nothing of the sort, she retorted. Why, Angus was looking forward to it all; it was his big day; he'd not miss it for a million Munchy bars.

'Yes, but last-minute stage fright . . .' suggested the sergeant.

'Well, all right then, where is he? Where do you go when you've got last-minute stage fright? You find him, then, for we can't!'

At last the sergeant asked if he could take a look round Angus's bedroom.

'He hasn't left a note, if that's what you're thinking.'

'But he might have left a clue.'

Mum, Dad, Kevin and the sergeant trooped upstairs, while Rosco sat howling on the back doorstep as if he knew that Angus was gone forever.

'His bed's been slept in, that's for sure!' cried Mrs Lang, flinging back the door to Angus's room.

'Aye, by a load of Olympic wrestlers,' added Dad, surveying the tortured sheets and blankets.

'H'm!' The sergeant stood for a moment, taking all in but saying nothing. At length he dived down to the bedside rug and tenderly gathered something up. It was a shred of pipe tobacco. Dropping this into one of the plastic bags he always carried, the sergeant turned to the Langs with a confident nod.

'I've never seen you with a pipe, Mr Lang. So either your son's a secret smoker, or he's been kidnapped.'

This made Kevin howl even louder than Rosco, until Mrs Lang took hold of him and shook him.

'Shut up, you big, spoilt baby!' she cried viciously. 'You're always on the moan!'

Chapter 8

At the Taste Gallery, a room had been set aside for
the presentation ceremony. There, in a fine gilt
frame, in the middle of a white wall, hung the
already famous 'Peace' of Angus Lang. Opposite
stood a television camera, whose crew were filling
in time with a few close-ups of the other pictures.
All around them seethed newspaper reporters with
their notebooks at the ready, Gallery officials, VIPs
and a few plain-clothes policemen. Sir Desmond
Snubbs, resplendent in a three-piece, pin-striped
suit with red carnation in its buttonhole, glanced
edgily at his watch for the umpteenth time. The
programme was supposed to be on the air. Could
there have been another rail strike? Could the taxi-
driver have lost his way? Could young Angus have
gone down with the measles at the last minute?
Nervously, Sir Desmond's fingers crept to his inside
pocket, checking upon the cheque as a best man
checks upon the ring. He drew forth an immaculate
white handkerchief with which he proceeded to
mop his distinguished brow—a gesture watched
eagerly by several million viewers. The ceremony
was twenty minutes late and the crowd was growing
restless. The radio commentator had described the
dresses of everyone in sight, including two charwom-

en who sneaked through the room on their way to their belated elevenses. At last, just when everyone was beginning to suspect the worst, a uniformed policeman appeared. He stood just inside the doorway, looking round. Then he spotted Sir Desmond Snubbs, went over to him and whispered in his ear. Sir Desmond's bushy white eyebrows shot up as he listened with obvious concern. Then he turned and whispered to the official standing next to him. The official whispered to someone else in turn, and gradually the whisper travelled round the room.

'It looks like the boy's been kidnapped!'

The television camera zoomed in on startled faces, the reporters surged, the VIPs twittered on their little gilt chairs like song-birds on golden perches. The plain-clothes policemen sidled furtively about, and the buzzing and twittering grew louder as imaginations practically burst into flames.

'Our live broadcast from the Taste Gallery has been interrupted by some very sensational news,' began the television commentator in a throbbing voice. 'It appears that the young boy prizewinner may have been kidnapped. We shall bring you further details as soon as they are available, but at the moment all we have are rumours. One of the rumours is that after all this sensational publicity, that "Peace" picture may soon be worth a fortune.

Well, as I say, we shall be standing by for further developments, but for the moment we return you to the studio . . . .'

This message bounced from Telstar right into the sitting-room of Cyrus J. Beefenberger, at his villa on Long Island, New York, USA. Cyrus was an art-collector of renown. In fact, at that very moment, without so much as turning his head, he could see two Van Goghs, a Renoir and a couple of Lowrys. Cyrus picked up his ruby-studded telephone.

'Get me my London agent.'

'Yes, Mr Beefenberger.'

'Fast!'

'Right away, Mr Beefenberger.'

'Harry? Is that you? Well now, listen here. You get over to the Taste Gallery right away—(do you hear me, Harry? The Taste Gallery, I said)—and make them an offer for a picture called "Peace", the one painted by some kid or other . . . .'

The line crackled.

'Sure I'm sure! Yeah, I know all about the competition and the kid and everything. It's my job to know every story about every work of art. And it's your job to do as you're told. I don't care how much you have to pay for it; I want that picture. Right?'

'Right, Mr Beefenberger. But—'

'The only butt I know is on one end of a rifle. So

47

just you go get me that picture, Harry. At the double.'

'Right away, Mr Beefenberger.'

Cyrus slammed down the telephone and turned his head a couple of centimetres to the left. He could now see one Leonardo da Vinci, two large Corots and an Epstein bust. He began to wonder where on earth he was going to hang the 'Peace' when it arrived. Maybe he'd have to throw a Constable away. Problems, problems!

Chapter 9

'It's so peaceful,' said Angus Lang dreamily, 'that I wish I could stay here for ever.'

'Far as I'm concerned you can,' replied Tom the bargee. 'One little 'un like you don't make much difference, and it's nice for me to have a bit of company. 'Specially somebody what appreciates the beauties o' nature. (I do believe I seen a kingfisher just then, back o' them trees.)'

Angus felt flabbergasted at such a carefree approach to life. Tom evidently didn't care tuppence what Angus's mother might think, or how Angus's schooling might suffer. He hadn't even thought about such mundane matters as clean socks, pyjamas or toothbrush, none of which Angus had remembered to bring with him. Angus concluded that none of these things must be really important. Yet he still wore his guilt like a great suit of wrong-size armour.

'My mum will be upset if I don't go home.'

'Do her good. She upset you, didn't she? And tried to spend your money before you'd even laid hands on it. Fair's fair, then. You can send her a postcard when we get to Liverpool.'

It sounded all right, but there was one thing which Tom hadn't thought of. One very important thing—and that was Rosco. Angus was very fond of that dog. He knew that he couldn't live long apart from Rosco, so there was no question of his staying on the barge for ever. On the other hand, he dreaded the thought of going back home whilst his mother was still in a fury. (He could well imagine her face and the sound of her voice when she found he'd disappeared.) So why not compromise? It was Friday. He could spend the weekend with Tom, then go back home on Monday morning, just in time to escape again to school. By then his mother would be so glad to see him—(having thought of him as dead)—that maybe she'd give him a big hug and double his spends. As for that rotten picture, perhaps the fuss would all die down when he didn't turn up for his prize. They could always give it to the runner-up; some girl from the Isle of Man, if he wasn't mistaken. Pity about the loss of the five hundred pounds, but of course it was never really his by rights, and Angus knew he'd never have been able to spend it the way he wanted, in any case. What was left of it.

'Fancy a spot of fishing?' asked Tom. 'There's a rod under that tarpaulin behind you. Let's see how you shape. There's half an hour or so before the next lock. Time to catch us a bite for our dinner.'

Angus was delighted. He'd been fishing with his friends a time or two, but had never possessed a rod

of his own. He took it out from its hiding place and stroked it lovingly. Then he worked out what to do, cast off his line and waited. Life was really beginning to be quite bearable.

Meanwhile, Cyrus J. Beefenberger's London agent, Harry, was rushing up the steps into the Taste Gallery. Here he discovered, in an eminent huddle in one of the offices, Sir Desmond Snubbs himself, and Mr Redford Ragg, the Chairman of the Peace-Among-Nations Inspirational Committee, PAN-IC.

'I don't really see,' Sir Desmond was saying, 'how I can be blamed for anything that has happened. I am merely giving back the cheque to you because I have been unable to hand it over to the winner.'

'Oh, don't misunderstand me!' cried Redford Ragg, 'Red' to his friends. 'It isn't a question of blame at all. On the contrary! The whole sad affair is—dare I say it?—wonderful publicity for our cause. Of course, we deplore—'

'Excuse me!' Harry interrupted. 'I'm looking for the Chairman of PANIC. Do you know if he's still in the building?'

'You're looking right at him,' Redford smiled. But Sir Desmond cut in coldly, 'No more reporters! We've had quite enough publicity for one day. Out you go, young man, and please close the door

behind you.'

Harry was not accustomed to being taken for a reporter. He felt offended, tried to express his indignation and was forcibly seized by Sir Desmond before he could explain. Sir Desmond was at the end of his tether. He felt he had been made to look foolish in public, and now he was being hounded by the press. His privacy was being invaded. He shook poor Harry so fiercely that Harry's new dental plate slipped out of position. Perhaps it was this which made him less articulate than usual, for when he did finally make himself heard, the other two could only chorus: 'WHAT DID YOU SAY?'

'I said,' repeated Harry, clicking his denture back into place, 'that my American client wishes to make an offer of 50,000 dollars for the "Peace" picture.'

Sir Desmond was astounded; Redford gaped, then repeated the figure in utter disbelief.

'All right then, a hundred thousand,' Harry urged.

'But you can't possibly . . . .'

'Two hundred thousand.'

'You seem to be under the mistaken impression . . . .'

'Five hundred thousand!'

'My dear chap, this is ridiculous!' Sir Desmond cried, mopping his brow, in his confusion, with a green felt pen-wiper from the desk behind him.

'All right then, one million dollars. How about that?'

Sir Desmond turned crimson; Redford Ragg turned greenish-grey. 'I don't believe it!' Redford croaked.

'Two million dollars!'

'No, don't say another word! You're breaking my heart. You see, the picture isn't mine to sell. It would have been if the lad had come forward and claimed his prize. He would have had the five hundred pounds, and we, in return, would have had the picture to use as we wanted. But he didn't turn up, so it still belongs to him.' Here Redford wobbled and had to sit down.

'We must find him, then, mustn't we?' cried Harry, already fearing the wrath of his American client. 'One little lad can't have got far away, all on his own.'

'He's probably been kidnapped,' Sir Desmond announced. 'In fact, the more I hear of this whole incredible episode, the more certain I am that he has been kidnapped. There's a great deal more to this than meets the eye.'

Chapter 10

By Saturday morning, Angus had learned a great deal about fishing. He had actually caught one or two small fish, but that was not really what mattered. The game was the thing.

"Course, there's nothing very big in this canal,' said Tom consolingly. But for once Tom was wrong. Not half an hour later, just as they were coming within sight of Waxford Lock, Angus felt a mighty pull on his line. Eyes gleaming triumphantly, he began to draw the fish in. He thought he had never felt so happy in the whole of his life.

The fish turned out to be a pike, and was a great deal stronger than Angus had imagined. There was a jerk, followed immediately by a stronger jerk, and suddenly, with a startled cry, Angus found himself diving head-first into the chilly black water, having left one of his shoes behind. The rod flew through the air and the pike escaped, dragging the rod down-water after him.

'Tom! Help! I'm drow . . . glug, glug!'

Tom was by this time on the far side of the barge, concentrating on the lock ahead, and on two idiots in a pleasure boat who were sailing far too fast towards him. In any case, though he would never admit it, Tom was more than a little deaf. The barge moved purposefully on, leaving Angus floundering wildly in the water.

The pleasure boat, now bearing down on Angus, was called *Molly*. A soppy name for a boat, as Simon Crickle had remarked to his friend Ferdie Flapp when they had first looked the vessel over.

'If you want to call it Goliath, or Jaws, or Pterodactyl, feel free,' Ferdie had replied, heaving his great, framed rucksack on board. 'Just so long as we get a nice, uneventful holiday.'

Simon and Ferdie were students fresh from examinations and more than ready for a spell of relaxation before the dreaded results. Yet 'uneventful' was to be the least appropriate word for their trip. Why, that very morning, not only had they stunned a duck, stalled the engine, almost capsized in Waxford Lock and been abused by some loud-mouthed bargee, but they had now spotted a body in the water.

'Man overboard!' yelled Ferdie, rushing for the boat-hook. He could be a man of action in a crisis, though he regarded himself primarily as a poet. (So far on this trip he had sat for hours with a notebook open on his lap, gazing at water, banks or sky with a bemused expression and occasionally sighing very deeply. Though after three days it must be admitted that his notebook was still open at page one.)

Simon flung down his guitar and rushed to

help . . . taking care however, to fling the instrument safely on to a pile of sacks. That guitar meant more to Simon than a plague to an undertaker. If Simon didn't manage a degree, then he would shoot to fame as a pop-star overnight. (In fact, there were times when Simon actually hoped and prayed that he would fail all his examinations.) Now, however, all thoughts of fame laid by, he dived into the water. Shuddering with shock in the painful cold, he struck out towards the dark shape snatching desperately at their wake.

Simon grabbed Angus and Ferdie grabbed Simon. Soon, they had hauled on board a wet, heavy, gasping, terrified young boy.

Although there was no need for anything as drastic as the kiss of life, the boy did look a sorry mess. His face was blotched, his hair was weedy and his clothes were sopping rags. What's more, a great big lump was rising where he must have caught the back of his head on something sharp. As a final indignity, he had only one shoe.

However, by the time this waif had been rolled up in a warm, dry towel and given a mug of hot cocoa, he began to look a little better.

'What's your name, son?'

'Er—' Angus eyed his captors furtively. 'I—I can't remember.'

'Were you on a boat?'

'Don't know.'

'Can't you remember anything?'

'Nope. Just feel this lump on the back of my head,' said Angus with more confidence.

Angus was put to bed in the spare bunk, then Simon and Ferdie withdrew to discuss what to do with him.

'Do you think he has lost his memory?'

'Could have, with a bump like that. But it's more likely he's up to something, and doesn't want us to find out.'

'What would you have been up to at that age? Running away from home?'

'Too true, if I'd had half a chance. Always kept my savings and a bar of chocolate ready, but somehow it never came off.'

'I managed it once,' mused Simon. 'Then some nosy old biddy saw me pinching the birds' crusts in the park, and handed me over to the police. They scared me half to death, they did.'

'Yeah, we won't do that to him. If we handle it right, we can persuade him to go home of his own free will.'

'You think?'

'Let's find out who he is first. One of us stay with the lad, the other go ashore for a local newspaper. If he's from round here, it'll say he's missing.'

'Better still, we could try the local pubs, ask a few

questions there.'

'What a good idea!' Ferdie beamed. 'I'll be off, then, right away.'

Chapter 11

'I tell you I saw young Angus at six o'clock yesterday morning,' the milkman said. 'He was running off across the fields towards the canal.'

'Well, why didn't you say so before?'

'Nobody asked me, that's why. I've been busy. I didn't even know the lad was missing.'

The police sergeant, who had been questioning the villagers for hours, felt at last that his patience had been rewarded. 'Nobody with him?'

'Not a soul about. Never is, at that time in the morning. Lovely and peaceful, as a rule.'

'Looks as though he might have fallen in the canal and drowned, then.'

'Well, for pity's sake don't go telling his mother that. She'll have a fit.'

'She'll soon find out why we're dragging the canal.'

'He can't swim either, young Angus can't.'

'Oh, dear! There's a tragedy for somebody every day . . . .'

'Here, just a minute!' interrupted the milkman's wife. 'I wonder if he was the lad I saw the other day, on Tom Heston's barge? Having the time of his life, he was, running up and down with bits of rope, and a face as black as coal.'

'Old Tom Heston wouldn't kidnap anybody. He's as mild and gentle as a baby's bath-suds.'

'Nobody said he'd kidnapped the lad. But he might have given him a ride.'

'H'm. I suppose it's worth a try,' said the sergeant, scribbling in his notebook. 'I could find out whether Tom's passed here today, and if he has, we'll have him followed up the canal and search his barge.'

They did. A police car drew up near Waxford Lock, just as Tom's barge had gone through.

"Morning, Mr Heston. Got a young helper with you today, I believe?'

'Maybe I have, maybe I haven't,' Tom said warily. If the police were asking questions, it looked as though young Angus was in some sort of trouble. Tom was certainly not going to be the one to betray him. He glanced cautiously about him. Angus was nowhere to be seen. The lad must have spotted the police car coming, and hidden himself somewhere.

'Mind if we take a look round, then?' One policeman was already leaping on board, and another looked ready to follow him.

'Yes, I do mind! I've got a load here has to be in Liverpool tomorrow. Can't hang about talking to you lot.'

'That's all right. Just carry on, Mr Heston, and we'll come with you. We'll get the car to pick us up further on.'

'What's up, then?' asked Tom cautiously.

'Lad missing. Thought he might have stowed away on board. You never know.'

'I know!' cried Tom indignantly. 'I know every inch of this barge. There's no lad stowed away on here.' By now, Tom had had a chance to cast his eye over the barge pretty thoroughly, and he could see that Angus was not there. The boy had very likely slipped quietly into the water to dodge his pursuers. Tom did not know that Angus could not swim, and he decided the best way he could help his young friend was to put as much distance between him and the police as possible.

'Look round if you like,' Tom grudgingly invited, as he furtively began to increase the barge's speed.

On the table in the little cabin was a dark brown leather pouch. The first policeman picked it up and sniffed it. Then he signalled to his companion. They opened the pouch, took out a pinch of tobacco which they dropped carefully into a plastic bag, then continued their search. Finally, half-hidden under a huge tarpaulin, they found a shoe. A boy's shoe with—(as school regulations insisted)—a name written carefully inside. The name was Angus Lang.

'If you'll just pull into the side as soon as convenient . . .' one policeman said to Tom.

'. . . We'll get somebody over right away to take

your load on to Liverpool,' finished the other.

Tom, normally so calm, grew quite alarmed. 'What's going on? Here, what are you doing with them handcuffs? What are you playing at? I ain't done nothing wrong.'

'We'll see about that at the station,' said the first policeman grimly.

Chapter 12

'"MILLIONAIRE" ANGUS STILL MISSING' shrieked the Saturday morning headlines. Even *The Times* and the *Guardian* ran the story as their lead. All had photographs of Angus, plucked eagerly from the family album by Mrs Lang, who vowed she would do anything to find her son, millionaire or not. She cried a lot as she told the reporters: 'His dad's out on strike, an' all. And you should see his little brother Kevin! He's that upset! And the dog's fretting something awful.'

'Of course,' commented Angus's dad with practical good sense, 'the lad's only a minor. If he doesn't turn up, then that picture belongs to me.'

What with the police, the newspapers, the television, the messages of sympathy and the nosy neighbours, Mrs Lang hadn't had such an exciting time for years. It was almost better than the trip to London would have been. Not that she wasn't grieving. Anyone who has come so close to a million pounds and not been able to lay hands on it will know exactly how she felt. As for Kevin, he was coming down with chicken pox, only nobody had time to notice.

The sensation of Angus Lang's disappearance looked like lasting for days, or even weeks. It seemed that only a major disaster, such as Star Wars really breaking out, could oust it from the headlines. Yet by Saturday lunchtime an even greater sensation had burst upon the news-hungry world. The 'Peace' picture had been stolen!

It seemed that just before Gallery opening time on Saturday morning, the night-watchman was found unconscious in a dark corner of the Taste Gallery with his key-bunch missing. There was an ominously bare patch on the wall where 'Peace' had hung, yet the alarm had never sounded. It had been expertly dismantled.

'Top grade professionals!' cried Sir Desmond Snubbs when he heard the news. 'Those villains knew exactly what they were looking for, and when and how to get it. That picture must be worth even more that we thought.'

'You can't help admiring their cheek,' said Redford Ragg ruefully.

The art world was rocked like an empty canoe going over Niagara Falls. There had been nothing like this since the Mona Lisa was attacked. Cables and telex messages flew back and forth like midges in a swamp, and all the ports and airports were alerted for the thieves. Had they grabbed not only the picture but its artist, too? Did they intend to keep young Angus prisoner, forcibly painting more and more pictures for them to sell? The whole thing

had become an International Incident. Questions were to be asked at the United Nations General Assembly as to whether the greed of the rich should be allowed to force up prices high enough to put children's lives at risk.

'The more famous and valuable that painting becomes, the less chance we have of finding that boy alive,' said a spokesman from the Save the Children fund.

Meanwhile, the battered night-watchman regained consciousness and started mumbling something about loose false teeth.

'You haven't got them in, love,' a kindly nurse assured him. 'Look, here they are, in this jar on top of your locker.'

Chapter 13

'Look, we know who you are,' said Simon Crickle kindly. 'Ferdie here has just been ashore to do a bit of research. It seems there's a great hue and cry on, and we think we'd better take you home.'

'No!' cried Angus in alarm.

'You haven't really lost your memory,' Ferdie grinned. 'I tried that once, at about your age, when I broke a jeweller's window with my football. But it's ever so easy to detect. You can't get away with it for more than an hour.'

'I have lost my memory,' Angus insisted. 'I've no idea how I came to be on this canal.'

'Oh, you do know it's a canal, then, and not some river?'

'Well, I'm guessing, aren't I?' Angus's cheeks turned pink.

'And I'm guessing your folks will be ever so glad to have you back.'

'No, they won't! They only want the money.'

Simon grinned. 'What money's that, then?'

Angus knew that he had given himself away, and the best thing to do seemed to be to burst into tears.

'Hey, cheer up! I've brought some fish and chips back with me.' Ferdie began unwrapping a great, greasy parcel, the smell of which was very tempting to a hungry, growing lad. Before he knew it, Angus had wiped his eyes on his blanket and started tucking in.

'We'll come with you and explain,' said Simon when the tale was told at last. 'We'll say you were so nervous of the presentation that you decided you daren't go through with it. After all, that's most of the truth.'

'My mum will kill me!'

'No, she won't. If you could see her now . . . .'

Eventually, the two students managed to persuade young Angus that they were right. After all, what else could he do? He couldn't stay with them for ever, and anyway, Ferdie had also brought back news of Tom's arrest. It was up to Angus to sort that out as soon as possible.

'All right; you win,' he told them without enthusiasm.

Angus had to borrow a pair of Ferdie's old track-shoes, since he had only one shoe of his own. The track-shoes were a couple of sizes too big, but when stuffed with newspapers they didn't seem too bad. Angus found he could shuffle along quite well. Then he put on some borrowed clothes and they set off. The three of them walked along the towpath until they came to a stile. This led into a field, which led to another field, which finally led to a road. By the roadside was a bus stop, and there they waited

for twenty minutes, until finally a lorry came along.

'You lot want a lift, then? Where you going?'

'Bordham,' said Ferdie. 'Only a little place. Do you know where it is?'

'Bordham? 'Course I do! It's the one with the nasty bend in the High Street. My pal's wheel come off there the other week, and he went slap through the Post Office window. Could've been nasty.'

With some misgivings, the trio clambered aboard, but they did not have long to worry. Almost immediately the driver diverted their thoughts with an exciting tale.

'Ain't half been some goings-on at Speke airport this morning, I can tell you. That's where I've just come from, Speke airport. Held me up for two hours, they did. Police swarming all over the place, looking for some art robbers or something.'

Angus's ears pricked up.

'Did they catch them?'

'I'll say they did! What a hullaballoo! Seems these robbers had chased up from London, thinking the London airports would more likely be watched, but the police come and stopped this plane, just when it was taxi-ing off to America. I saw 'em drag this bloke down the steps and off that plane like he was a sack of turnips late for a royal banquet. Dragged him so bloomin' rough his false teeth fell out.'

'What about the picture?' asked Angus breathlessly.

'Still had it under his arm in a canvas bag. But that wasn't all, not half! This bloke was supposed to have kidnapped some kid or other, as well. They searched the plane, searched all the airport, toilets, waiting-rooms, store-rooms, vehicles, my lorry . . . thought I'd be there till next Christmas.'

'Quite a carry-on!' remarked Ferdie, winking at Simon. 'I'm glad we're not mixed up in it.'

Angus groaned. 'How long will it take us to get back to Bordham?' He looked so impatient all of a

sudden that you'd have thought he had an ice-cream sundae waiting there, melting away before he could get a spoon to it.

Chapter 14

Mrs Lang threw her arms around her son and almost squashed him flat. As for Rosco, he leaped and barked and nearly went berserk.

'Oh, Angus! My lamb! My baby! My treasure!' cried Mrs Lang with exaggerated passion, yet spilling quite genuine tears.

'Hello, Mum!' Angus muttered anxiously, trying to wriggle free to give Rosco a cuddle. It was only a matter of time, he felt, before his mother's mood changed back to normal. Meantime, he had to admit it was quite nice to have a fuss made over him.

At length, Mrs Lang dried her eyes and stood back to admire her offspring. It was then she noticed the strange assortment of garments in which Angus was dressed. A too-big sweater of Ferdie's; Simon's oldest jeans, rolled up at the bottoms and taken in at the waist with safety-pins; and the track-shoes stuffed with paper.

'Grief and sorrow! You look like a walking jumble-sale! What's happened to your good school uniform?'

'It's all right, Mrs Lang.' Simon produced a large parcel in a damp plastic bag. 'His own clothes are here. They got a bit wet, so we lent him some of

ours, not wanting him to catch cold. If you hang them up in the kitchen they'll soon dry off.'

'Wet?' Mrs Lang put a wealth of meaning into that one word. 'But it hasn't rained all week.'

'Here we go!' thought Angus resignedly. Things were promising to slip back to normal even more quickly than he'd imagined. He went and buried his head in Rosco's shaggy coat.

But Mrs Lang knew her manners. Further questions must wait. These two young men, however scruffy they might look, had brought her son back to her, and they must be given a cup of tea. She bustled about, setting a tray with the best cups and saucers, and even producing a plate of coconut pyramids, left over from the cancelled trip. And all the time she chattered on, mostly of how upset she'd been, and what a sensation it had all caused, and the way she'd searched, and wept, and broken her heart, and vowed she'd do anything to get Angus back.

'I suppose you know your picture got stolen? And some poor old night-watchman got bumped on the head as well? Anyway, you needn't worry, son, the policeman just came to tell me they've got it back. He'd just had a phone call from Liverpool, it seems. They stopped some villain at the airport, trying to fly off to America with your picture, if you please!' She turned to Simon and Ferdie. 'It's a lovely picture, you know. He's quite an artist, our Angus.'

'Did they have it with them, Mum? Did they give it you?'

'What, the picture? Oh no, not yet. It's still in Liverpool, and it has to be gone over for finger-prints and the like. Policeman said it would be a week or two before they handed it back. And I want to talk to you about that.'

'I've got to go and see the police, Mum. Right away. I've got stuff to tell them.' Angus, keen to change the subject, had guessed what his mother was going to say.

'It can wait five minutes, surely. You've not even said hello to our Kevin yet, and him in bed with chicken pox. Now, about that picture. I want you to take it out of the competition.'

'Eh?' said Angus rudely.

'You know why! You knew the rules as well as I did, right from the start.' But in case he had forgotten, she picked up a sheet of paper and started reading from it. 'Any prizewinning picture will belong to PANIC, to use as they please for the promotion of their cause.'

'Yes, well, that's okay by me,' said Angus. 'It always was.'

Mrs Lang cast her eyes up to Heaven. 'This lad wants his head seeing to,' she told the others. 'If his picture stays in the competition, he wins five hun-

dred pounds, and that's all. If he withdraws it, and sells it himself, he could be a millionaire. Did you hear what that American chap was offering—?'

'Five hundred pounds will do me nicely,' said Angus stoutly. 'I'd rather PANIC had the million. It's time somebody did something for a bit of peace.'

The fairy tale feeling crept over him again, though this time it was more of a Jack-the-Giant-Killer sensation. Angus had power at last, and he was going to use it properly.

'PANIC could do a lot of good with that money, Mrs Lang,' agreed Simon.

'They'd waste it. Anway, even if they didn't waste

it, what good is one little million pounds to set the whole world to rights?'

'It's a start, that's what,' said Ferdie. 'You've got to start somewhere. And think of the publicity, all for peace!'

Mrs Lang regarded the two students suspiciously. 'I do believe you two belong to that crazy lot yourselves. Well, you're not going to make us change our minds.'

'My mind's made up,' declared Angus even more stoutly. 'And it is my picture. Money's not everything,' he added, astonished to find that he believed it.

'I never heard such selfish cheek in all my life! Here we are, up to our necks in mortgages and hire-purchases, and our Kevin wanting a new trike and I don't know what, and your dad out on strike . . . .'

Just then the front door flew open and in marched Mr Lang, bristling with indignation.

'Sold down the river!' he shouted before he had even spotted his son. 'Strike's over. We're going back on Monday.'

'Hi, Dad! What does "sold down the river" mean?' asked Angus, rushing to meet his father.

'It means they've come to their senses at last,' said Mrs Lang with satisfaction. 'Just as you will when you've drunk that cup of tea and thought properly about what I've said.'

Chapter 15

The next sensation was that the art thief who had been captured on the plane escaped from custody on his way to jail. What's more, despite a thorough search, the man was never found, although of course the police still had the picture safe and sound.

It was almost a month before the picture was returned to the Taste Gallery, so that the presentation ceremony could be organised afresh. Nothing would shake Angus Lang's resolve to leave his picture in the competition, and he had even made up his mind that this time he would really go along to the presentation and get it over with. That seemed the only way to ensure that PANIC would have its chance to sell the picture and grow rich. To Angus's surprise, his dad supported him.

'We're not cut out to be millionaires,' he said after a deal of thought. 'You read of folks who've won the pools, and then had a right old miserable time of it—thousands of begging letters, and sponging friends, and too much drinking and gambling and carrying on. Let's just be thankful we've got our lad back, and done our bit for a better future.'

Two against one. Mrs Lang had to give in, though she intended to say 'I told you so!' for the rest of her life, whenever they happened to be short of money. On the other hand, she suddenly found she was proud of her son's unselfishness, which she began to stretch to include herself. 'We're doing it for the best for everybody,' she told the neighbours grandly. 'There's many a one would have snatched at all they could get, but not this family! We'll manage quite well by our own efforts, thank you very much!'

As the Presentation Day came round again, there was much the same bustle of preparation. This time, though, as Mr Lang was now earning again, and as the occasion looked like being a hundred times more newsworthy, Mrs Lang invested in a biscuit-coloured two-piece outfit with matching straw hat, which really looked quite smart. What's more, she had her hair done properly at the hair-dresser's.

In the end, five of them travelled to London together, Mr Lang having been granted a special day off work, and Tom the bargee having also been invited along, at Angus's insistence and expense. It seemed the least he could to to make up for the indignity that Tom had suffered that Saturday morning.

Not only did the little party take a taxi, with no thought of cost, but young Kevin wasn't sick at all, in spite of having eaten two sausage rolls, a cream bun and a monster bag of Chipples on the train.

Sir Desmond Snubbs was a trifle edgy, remembering the previous occasion and the violent events that had followed. But he looked every bit as smart, this time with a red rose in his buttonhole, and his speech was even better rehearsed than before. For this time there were even two Lords and a Royal in the audience, and the news had just come through that the 'Peace' picture was to be used as a postage-stamp illustration. If only that boy turned up!

Angus did turn up, ten minutes early, and was immediately pinned into a corner by a make-up lady who proceeded to comb his hair in a different direction, and dab at his face with a great, tickly powder-puff. Then his jacket was given a brush, his tie was straightened, his shirt-collar smoothed, his socks pulled up, until he began to look quite human. At last he was led forth, to stand on a special little dais in front of his picture, face to face with the great Sir Desmond Snubbs.

It was a stomach-churning moment. There was the television camera, moving steadily, relentlessly, towards him. There was the radio commentator prattling away quietly into his microphone. There were the crowds, the VIPs sitting on their little gilt chairs, the newspaper reporters and their cameramen, the private detectives clustered round the Royal, art critics, posh onlookers and his mum,

dad, Kevin and Tom. Tom winked, but Angus wasn't looking. He had fixed his eyes firmly on his feet. A hush descended. Sir Desmond cleared his throat.

'Your Royal Highness, my Lords, Ladies and Gentlemen . . . .' The presentation had begun!

As Sir Desmond took off into his speech, which was by no means short, Angus plucked up the courage to lift his eyes and stare around him. He soon wished he hadn't, for the sight of all those well-dressed people and those popping flash-blubs and those earphoned, shirt-sleeved cameramen, was enough to terrify a tiger. He turned his eyes away again and glanced instead at the wall behind him, where his picture had pride of place. It stood out a few inches from the wall, because behind it a special alarm had been installed. Angus could see well-disguised wires running hither and thither, and could not help feeling proud that people had gone to all this trouble over his little work of art.

And then he froze. He had spotted something else; something very strange indeed, which was nothing to do with the wires or the security or even the presentation ceremony. It was the picture of 'Peace' itself. There was something wrong with it!

Suddenly, in the middle of one of Sir Desmond's nicely rounded sentences, Angus yelled: 'Hey, that's not my picture! There should be a big black blob on the end of the nose. It's a fake, a copy, a forgery!'

Far away, in a villa on Long Island, Cyrus J. Beefenberger, who was watching the programme live, began to chuckle. Propped against his arm-chair was a Constable in a massive gold frame, which he had had to take down to make room for his latest acquisition.

'Peace, perfect peace!' he sighed contentedly.

Unlike Mr Lang, who was remarking at that very

moment to an excited newspaper reporter: 'There'll be no peace now until she's started World War Three over that dratted picture!'

THE SIEGE OF COBB STREET SCHOOL

Hazel Townson

When gunmen burst in and hold their class hostage, Lenny and Jake are hiding in the cloakroom having a sneaky bag of crisps — and that's how they manage to escape.

But what are they to do? Will they be able to get in touch with people outside the school to warn them of what is happening? Can they outwit the gunmen and rescue their friends?

'Told with great gusto and will delight readers of primary school age who like plenty of action' *Junior Bookshelf*

REBECCA'S WORLD

Terry Nation

Rebecca, mysteriously transported to a distant planet through her father's astral telescope, sets out on an exciting adventure to the Forbidden Lands in search of the last Ghost tree.

This is a rich and often funny fantasy for younger readers by Terry Nation, the creator of the Daleks.

'Undoubtedly the funniest, most imaginative children's book to have appeared in many years.'

London Evening News

If you're an eager Beaver reader, perhaps you ought to try some more of our exciting titles. They are available in bookshops or they can be ordered directly from us. Just complete the form below and enclose the right amount of money and the books will be sent to you at home.

☐	THE SUMMER OF THE WAREHOUSE	Sally Bicknell	£1.25
☐	THE GOOSEBERRY	Joan Lingard	£1.25
☐	FOX CUB BOLD	Colin Dann	£1.50
☐	GHOSTLY AND GHASTLY	Barbara Ireson Ed.	£1.50
☐	WHITE FANG	Jack London	£1.25
☐	JESS AND THE RIVER KIDS	Judith O'Neill	£1.50
☐	A PATTERN OF ROSES	K. M. Peyton	£1.25
☐	YOU TWO	Jean Ure	£1.50
☐	SNOWY RIVER BRUMBY	Elyne Mitchell	£1.25

If you would like to hear more about Beaver Books, and discover all the latest news, don't forget the BEAVER BULLETIN. If you just send a stamped self-addressed envelope to Beaver Books, Brookmount House, 62-65 Chandos Place, Covent Garden, London WC2N 4NW, we will send you the latest BULLETIN.

If you would like to order books, please send this form, and the money due to:

HAMLYN PAPERBACK CASH SALES, PO BOX 11, FALMOUTH, CORNWALL, TR10 9EN.

Send a cheque or postal order, and don't forget to include postage at the following rates: UK: 55p for first book, 22p for second, 14p thereafter; BFPO and Eire: 55p for first book, 22p for second, 14p per copy for next 7 books, 8p per book thereafter; Overseas: £1.00 for first book, 25p thereafter.

NAME ....

ADDRESS ....

....

Please print clearly

If you're an eager Beaver reader, perhaps you ought to try some more of our exciting titles. They are available in bookshops or they can be ordered directly from us. Just complete the form below and enclose the right amount of money and the books will be sent to you at home.

☐	HELLO MR TWIDDLE	Enid Blyton	85p
☐	THE ENCHANTED WOOD	Enid Blyton	95p
☐	THE MAGIC FARAWAY TREE	Enid Blyton	95p
☐	HEIDI'S SONG		95p
☐	URSULA BEAR	Sheila Lavelle	75p
☐	NICHOLAS ON HOLIDAY	Goscinny and Sempé	95p
☐	EMIL IN THE SOUP TUREEN	Astrid Lindgren	95p
☐	LOLLIPOP	Christine Nostlinger	£1.25
☐	THE WORST KIDS IN THE WORLD	Barbara Robinson	95p
☐	THE BROWNIES IN HOSPITAL	Pamela Sykes	95p
☐	THE GREAT ICE CREAM CRIME	Hazel Townson	85p
☐	THE MILL HOUSE CAT	Marjorie Ann Watts	£1.00
☐	BOGWOPPIT	Ursula Moray Williams	95p

And if you would like to hear more about Beaver Books, and find out all the latest news, don't forget the BEAVER BULLETIN. Just send a stamped, self-addressed envelope to Beaver Books, Brookmount House, 62-65 Chandos Place, Covent Garden, London WC2N 4NW.

If you would like to order books, please send this form, and the money due to:

HAMLYN PAPERBACK CASH SALES, PO BOX 11, FALMOUTH, CORNWALL TR10 9EN.

Send a cheque or postal order, and don't forget to include postage at the following rates: UK: 55p for first book, 22p for the second, 14p thereafter; BFPO and Eire: 55p for first book, 22p for the second, 14p per copy for next 7 books, 8p per book thereafter; Overseas £1.00 for first book, 25p thereafter.

NAME...

ADDRESS...

....

Please print clearly